E · ESTOU AQUI · EST

SUIS LÀ · TÔI ĐÂY

Í · WAA IK··· · A

ÍN DA · ÉG ER HÉR

OU II · I'M HERE ·

A HUNA · JE SUI

To those who were here before us, those we welcome today, and those arriving in the future. To our children: Beckett, Reuben, and Sabo. And to our beloved pile of friends, collaborators, and co-conspirators. Here for you, always.

—Jennifer & Miry

To those who strive to live their lives by the Golden Rule. May we continue to be intentional in being a good neighbor to those around us, to those in our community, and in our world.

—Nomar Perez

Text © 2022 by Miry Whitehill and Jennifer Jackson
Illustrations © 2022 by Nomar Perez
Cover and internal design © 2022 by Allison Sundstrom/Sourcebooks
Sourcebooks and the colophon are registered trademarks of Sourcebooks.
Photoshop was used to prepare the full color art.
Published by Sourcebooks eXplore, an imprint of Sourcebooks Kids
P.O. Box 4410, Naperville, Illinois 60567-4410
(630) 961-3900
sourcebookskids.com
Cataloging-in-Publication Data is on file with the Library of Congress.
Source of Production: Worzalla, Stevens Point, Wisconsin, USA
Date of Production: December 2021
Run Number: 5023876
Printed and bound in the United States of America.
WOZ 10 9 8 7 6 5 4 3 2 1

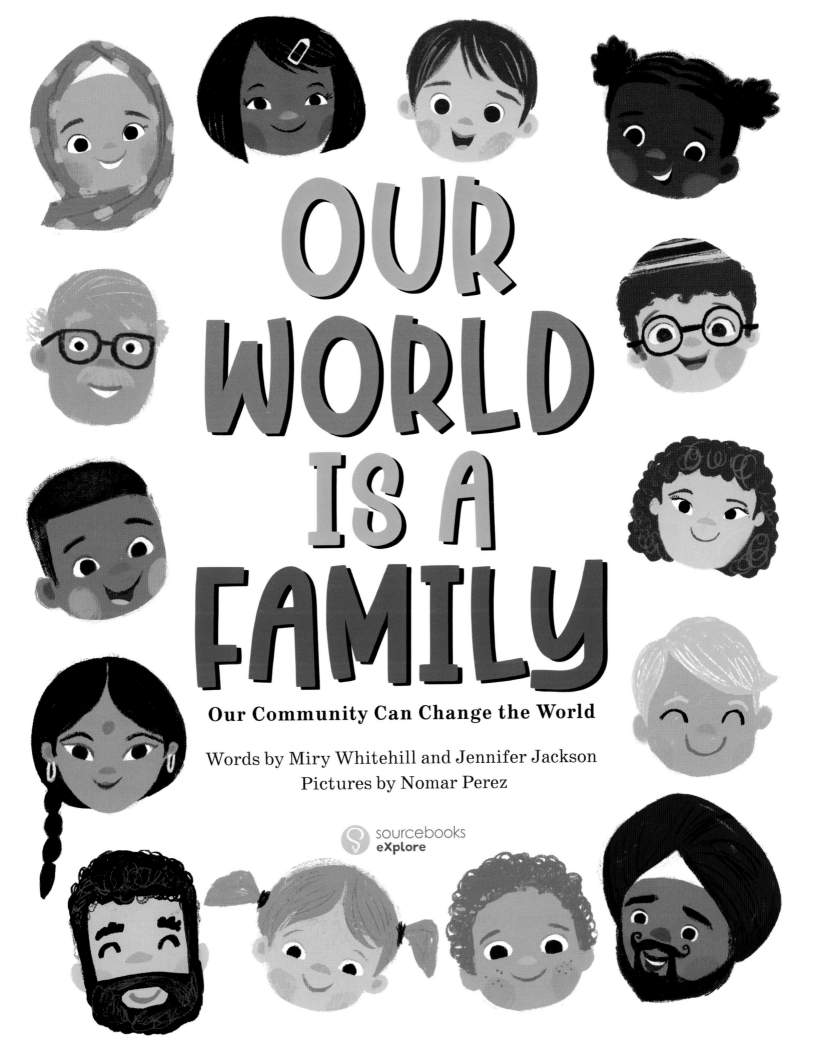

OUR WORLD IS A FAMILY

Our Community Can Change the World

Words by Miry Whitehill and Jennifer Jackson
Pictures by Nomar Perez

sourcebooks
eXplore

Our great, blue planet is bigger than you can even imagine.

Wherever we find land and plants,
we find people and animals,
living and growing and making a home.

There are more types of people than you ever thought possible.
They live in cold places,

hot places,

big cities,

and small towns.

All around the world, people speak different languages.

No matter what language they speak, people everywhere want to feel safe and loved and important.

But there are places in the world where it stops being safe for people to live.

Sometimes it becomes so unsafe that children can't go to school and parents can't go to work and no one can play outside. When that happens, people might need to leave home and move to a new part of the world.

They might move by foot, by bus, or by plane.

They might travel a very long way to find a place
where it is safe and quiet.

When they finally arrive, they might miss their old home.
Maybe they had to leave behind special things.

And special people.

Maybe their new home doesn't feel like home at all.

When we see someone new in our neighborhood, how can we help them feel safe and loved and important? How can we tell them you're not alone?

There are so many ways! You can start by saying it with a smile.

You can say it with a hand.

You can say it with a gift.

Or you can just say, "I'm here."

ICH BIN DA

ESTOY AQUÍ

WAA IKAN

ANA HUNA

HINENI

JE SUIS LÀ

Before you know it, you'll think of even more ways to help your new neighbors feel at home.

You could share a cup of tea.

Build important things together.

Cook a delicious new food.

Learn to say "I love you" in a new language.

Hug and dance and play if you want—you won't need any words at all!

And there, safe in their new home,
children can go to school,
parents can go to work,

and everyone can play outside. Together.

People live all over our big, blue world.
And together, we'll find a place for everyone.

A note to readers:

Thank you for taking a proactive role in learning about migration. We want to support you having honest, age-appropriate conversations about why people move around the world as refugees. For more resources and to explore this important topic, visit miryslist.org/ourworldisafamily

Love,
Miry & Jennifer

ER HERNA·I'M HE

ANA HUNA· JE

ÉRNA · ESTOY AQU

E·TÔI ĐÂY·ICH B

TOU AQUÍ· LEA UA

LÀ·I'M HERE·AN